Meet the Avengers

written by Michael Teitelbaum

based on the Marvel comic book series *The Mighty Avengers*

interior illustrated by Pat Olliffe and Hi-Fi Design

Reader's Digest
Children's Books®

New York, New York • Montréal, Québec • Bath, United Kingdom

Here come the Avengers.

1

The Avengers are a team of the world's greatest Super Heroes. They battle super villains and use their incredible powers to protect Earth. But who are the mighty heroes that make up the Avengers?

CAPTAIN AMERICA

Small and weak, Steve Rogers was given the Super-Soldier serum. The serum made him incredibly strong and fast. He decided to call himself Captain America and became the first Avenger. He is a brilliant leader who comes up with plans to help the Avengers defeat their enemies.

Captain America has a super-strong shield that can slice through almost anything. When Captain America throws his shield it always comes back to him.

② ③ ④

Super Hero Name:
Captain America

Real Name: Steve Rogers

Height: 6 ft. 2 in.
Weight: 220 lbs
Eye Color: Blue
Hair Color: Blond

Abilities/Powers:
- Superior physical strength
- Incredible agility
- Exceptional endurance
- Superior intelligence
- Advanced combat skills

Weapons: Shield

Enemy: Red Skull

Weakness: No known weaknesses

Fun Fact: Captain America is less of a crime fighter and more of a world protector.

ANT-MAN

    Ant-Man was one of the first heroes to join the Avengers. He was a scientist who invented a formula that allowed him to change his size. As Ant-Man, he can shrink himself down to the size of an insect. Ant-Man can also communicate with insects and command them to help battle his enemies.

    Using his size-changing formula, Ant-Man can also grow very big. When he increases his size, he calls himself Giant-Man.

⑤

⑥

⑦

STATS

Super Hero Name:
Ant-Man/Giant-Man

Real Name: Henry "Hank" Pym

Height: 6 ft.
Weight: 190 lbs.
Eye Color: Blue
Hair Color: Reddish blond

Ability (when Henry Pym):
- Scientific genius

Abilities / Powers:
- Superior physical strength
- Ability to shift size from 1/2 an inch to over 100 feet tall
- Superior agility
- Superior endurance
- Ability to communicate with ants and other insects

Enemies: Ultron, Whirlwind

Weakness: No known weaknesses

Fun Fact: When he is the size of an ant, Ant-Man still keeps his human-size strength.

THE WASP

Ant-Man's partner is the Wasp. Just like Ant-Man, she can shrink down to the size of an insect.

8 She can also fly. The Wasp controls the electrical energy in her body to create blasts that sting her enemies. She calls these blasts her "stingers." The Wasp may be tiny, but she is a powerful hero and a valuable member of the Avengers.

STATS

Super Hero Name:
The Wasp

Real Name: Janet Van Dyne

Height: 5 ft. 4 in.
Weight: 110 lbs.
Eyes Color: Blue
Hair Color: Auburn

Ability (when Janet Van Dyne):
- Scientific genius

Abilities / Powers:
- Superior physical strength
- Ability to shrink to the size of an ant
- Great leadership skills
- Great fighting skills

Weapons: Wrist stingers with electric current

Enemies: Ultron, Whirlwind

Fun Fact: The Wasp came up with the name Avengers for the team.

THE HULK

When scientist Bruce Banner was caught in the explosion of a Gamma Bomb, the radiation changed his body. Now, whenever he gets angry, Dr. Banner turns into a huge green being known as the Hulk.

The Hulk is incredibly strong. Although he can't fly, the Hulk can leap hundreds of miles in one jump. The powerful Hulk can smash through just about anything!

STATS

Super Hero Name: The Hulk

Real Name: Bruce Banner

Height: 7 ft. (when Hulk)
Weight: 1040 lbs.
Eye color: green
Hair color: green

Ability (when Bruce Banner):
- Genius-level intellect in gamma radiation science

Abilities / Powers:
- Superhuman physical strength
- Superhuman speed
- Hulk Thunderclap
- Ability to travel hundreds miles in a single leap
- Strength increases with anger
- Accelerated healing

Enemies: Abomination, Absorbing Man, Loki, Hulk Busters

Weakness: Difficulty controlling rage

Fun Fact: Bruce's transformation into the Hulk can take anywhere from 25 seconds to 5 minutes.

THOR

Born in the magical realm of Asgard, the Mighty Thor is the God of Thunder. On Earth, he joined the Avengers to help stop his evil brother Loki.

Thor carries a mighty hammer that enables him to fly through the skies. He can even create thunder and lightning by striking it on the ground.

Thor also uses his hammer as a weapon. No matter where he throws it, the hammer always returns to Thor's hand.

STATS

Super Hero Name:
Thor Odinson

Earth Name: Donald Blake

Height: 6 ft. 6 in.
Weight: 640 lbs.
Eye Color: Blue
Hair Color: Blond

Abilities / Powers:
- Superhuman physical strength
- Flight (with the help of his hammer)
- Superhuman speed
- Incredible agility
- Able to summon thunder and lightning with the help of his hammer

Weapon: Hammer

Enemies: Loki, Kurse

Weakness: Losing his hammer

Fun Fact: Thor's Hammer, also known as Mjolnir, was formed from a collapsed star.

IRON MAN

(6)   Iron Man looks like a robot, but he is actually a man named Tony Stark.

(7)   After suffering a serious injury, Tony, a brilliant inventor, built himself a robotic suit to help keep him alive.

(8)   With the suit on he is Iron Man. The armor gives him incredible strength and powers. It allows him to fly and protects him from attacks. Iron Man can also fire blasts from his hands.

STATS

Super Hero Name: Iron Man

Real Name: Tony Stark

Height: 6 ft. 1 in.
Weight: 185 lbs.
Eye Color: Blue
Hair Color: Black

Ability (when Tony Stark):
- Genius-level intellect
- Inventor

Abilities/Powers:
- Superhuman strength
- Supersonic flight speed
- State-of-the-art Stark technology

Weapons: Energy repulsor blasts, hi-tech missiles, laser torch

Enemies: The Mandarin, Whiplash, Titanium Man

Weakness: Not having his Iron Man suit available

Fun Fact: Tony's Iron Man suit protects his heart and is powered by a computer.

Each hero is strong.

But together they are even stronger.
They are the Avengers!